The 100th Day
of School

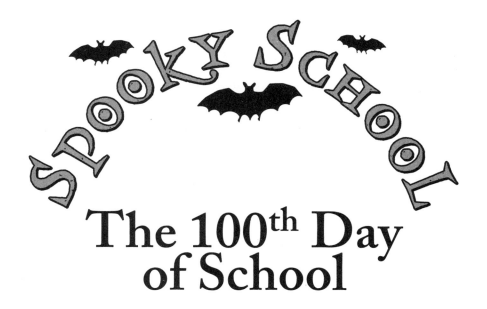

SPOOKY SCHOOL

The 100th Day of School

BONNIE BADER AND TRACEY WEST
ILLUSTRATIONS BY ALBERT MOLNAR

SCHOLASTIC INC.

New York   Toronto   London   Auckland   Sydney
Mexico City   New Delhi   Hong Kong

ISBN 0-439-21554-4

Text copyright © 2001 by Bonnie Bader and Pure West Productions. Illustrations copyright © 2001 by Scholastic Inc.

Book design by Steven Scott

12 11 10 9 8 7 6 5 4 3 2 1   1 2 3 4 5/0

Printed in the U.S.A.
First Scholastic printing, January 2001

CONTENTS

CHAPTER ONE

Howls and Fangs

"Good morning, class," said Ms. Batley. "Welcome to the 100th day of school!"

We all clapped.

My teacher stood in front of the class. She wore a long black dress. A bat necklace hung around her neck.

"I can't wait to see your presentations about the number one hundred," Ms. Batley said. "I'm sure they will be wonderful."

Ms. Batley smiled. She was very nice.

When I first met Ms. Batley, I was afraid of her. I thought she was a vampire. She sure looked like one.

I also thought the principal was a mad scientist. And the kids in school were monsters.

Things were a little better since my first day of school. Sure, things were still a bit strange. But everyone was friendly.

I was excited about the 100th day of school. I brought in my collection of favorite things.

I brought in twenty-five of my best marbles, twenty-five seashells I found on the beach, twenty-five cool rocks from all over the world, and twenty-five bows of different colors. I kept them in four separate boxes.

They were my most favorite things. I couldn't wait to show them to the class. *Today is going to be fun,* I thought.

Boy, was I wrong. I should have known. Nothing ever goes right in my spooky school!

It all started when Ms. Batley asked us to give our presentations. She called on Wally Wolfson first.

"What do you have in store for us, Wally?" Ms. Batley asked.

"I call this 'One Hundred Howls,'" Wally said.

One hundred howls? What does that mean? I wondered.

Then Wally started howling.

"*Awoooooooo!* One," Wally began. "*Awoooooooo! Two . . .*"

I wanted to cover my ears. The howls sounded like wolf howls.

Or werewolf howls.

I always thought Wally might be a werewolf. He had shaggy brown hair. And hairy arms.

Wally howled and howled.

"*Awooooo!* Ninety-nine," Wally said finally. "And now for my big finish."

Oh, no! I thought. Was he going to eat us? I looked for a way to escape the classroom.

"AaaaaaaWHOOOOOOOOO!" Wally's 100th howl was the loudest howl yet.

The class clapped and cheered.

"Wonderful, Wally!" said Ms. Batley. "Who will go next?"

Dave Draco raised his hand. "I brought in my collection, Ms. Batley," he said.

"Splendid," said our teacher. "Please come to the front of the room."

I couldn't believe Dave had a collection, too. I got nervous. What if it was just like mine?

I should not have worried. Dave had the strangest collection ever.

Dave straightened his red bow tie. He opened up a shiny metal case. Inside were rows and rows of tiny white things.

"This is my collection of teeth," Dave said. He held up a thick, square tooth. "I have twenty molars. These are the teeth that sit in the back of your mouth."

He held up a small, pointy tooth.

"I have twenty canine teeth," Dave said. "I have twenty front teeth. These are called incisors. And I have twenty bicuspids. They're like molars."

Finally, Dave held up a long, sharp tooth.

"I also have twenty fangs," Dave said. "That's five groups of twenty teeth. Five groups of twenty equal one hundred!"

Ms. Batley leaned over the box. "Very good, Dave," she said. "But I only count eighteen fangs, not twenty."

Dave smiled. His two pointy fangs gleamed white. "The last two are mine," Dave said.

The class laughed. But I didn't. Dave's fangs made him look just like a vampire.

I always thought Dave might be a vampire. Now I was more sure than ever. Who else would have a collection of fangs?

Dave sat down. His desk is next to mine. He smiled again. I could see his fangs.

"What's in the boxes?" he asked. "Do you have a collection, too?"

I opened the box of marbles. "I'm showing one hundred of my favorite things," I told him.

"Hazel, why don't you go next?" Ms. Batley asked.

Hazel sat in front of me. She wore a black dress, like always. She carried a broom. Her eyeglasses were shaped like cat eyes.

I always thought Hazel might be a witch. I wondered what she would do. Maybe she had a wart collection. Or maybe she would turn me into 100 frogs. I sank down into my seat.

Hazel stood in front of the class. She smoothed her long red braids.

"I'm going to read a poem about the number one hundred," Hazel said. "I wrote it myself."

Hazel was also the best student in class. Sometimes she liked to show off a little.

Hazel cleared her throat.

Twenty-five eyeballs rolling on the floor,
Twenty-five ghostly hands knocking on the door,

Hazel began. She recited the poem in a low, spooky voice. She seemed to be looking right at me.

It was too creepy. I looked away. The box of marbles was on my desk.

There was one problem.

They didn't look like marbles anymore. They looked like eyeballs. Slimy, gooey eyeballs.

I gasped. The eyeballs jumped out of the box. They rolled across the floor.

"*Eeeeek!*" I yelled.

CHAPTER TWO

Spideos?

"*Eeeek! Eeeek! Eeeek!*" I screamed again and again. "Jane," Ms. Batley said. "Whatever is the matter?"

"Eyeballs," was all I could say. I pointed to the floor. I heard some of the kids in the class giggling.

"Yes, Jane," Ms. Batley said. "Hazel already said eyeballs. Twenty-five eyeballs. Is something wrong, or can Hazel go on?"

Hazel still stood in front of the classroom. Her arms were folded. She did not look happy that I had interrupted her poem.

I looked down at the floor. My marbles were rolling away. *Marbles*, not *eyeballs*. What was I thinking? Or seeing? I rubbed my eyes.

"S-sorry," I said. I bent down to look for my twenty-five marbles. But they had all rolled away. What was I going to do now? I only had seventy-five things left in my collection. Ms. Batley was not going to like this.

Just then the lunch bell rang. Good. Hopefully, I could figure out what to do during lunch.

"Hazel, you can finish your poem when we get back to the classroom," Ms. Batley said.

When we got to the lunchroom, everyone ran to find a seat. Usually I sit with Dave, Wally, Hazel, and Glenda Specter. But I did not want to sit there today. Hazel was probably angry with me for ruining her presentation.

As I was looking around for a seat, I heard someone call my name. It was Hazel. *Oh, no,* I thought. She was going to give it to me now!

But when I looked over at Hazel, she was smiling. She wanted me to sit with her. *Phew!*

I sat down and took my sandwich out of my lunch bag.

Wally leaned over and sniffed my sandwich. "It smells funny," he said.

I shrugged. "It's just peanut butter and jelly," I told him.

"That sounds good," Hazel said. "Want to trade?"

I looked at Hazel's lunch. It looked like a normal sandwich. But it probably wasn't. Once she gave me a half and when I took a bite, it screamed! Or at least I thought it did.

I shook my head. "No, thanks," I said.

I looked over at Dave. He was pulling a bunch of little bags out of his lunch box.

"What are you doing, Dave?" I asked.

"My mom really got into this 100th day of school thing," Dave said. "She packed me ten bags of Spideos with ten Spideos in each bag — one hundred in all."

Spideos? I wondered. *What are they?* I picked up one of the bags. The Spideos looked like little round pieces of cereal. Black pieces of cereal. With — *legs*?!

I dropped the bag onto the table.

"It's okay, Jane," Dave said. "There's a bag for you. In fact, there's enough for each of us to have two bags."

Two bags? That meant twenty little spiders crawling around my lunch!

"N-no, thanks," I said. "I think I'm allergic to Spideos."

Dave shrugged and handed out the bags to the other kids.

Suddenly, I heard a strange knocking sound.

I looked around. Nothing. But the knocking did not stop. In fact, it was getting louder and louder.

I jumped up.

"What's wrong, Jane?" Wally asked.

"Do you hear a knocking sound?" I asked her.

Wally shook his head no.

But then I heard the sound again. And again! And again! It was driving me crazy. Where was that sound coming from?

I looked under the table. The sound was coming from my collection. I picked up my box of bows. Nothing. I picked up my box of seashells. Nothing. I picked up my box of rocks. And I heard the knocking sound! What was going on?

I looked at my friends. They were all busy eating

their Spideos. Hazel looked over at me and smiled. It was sort of a strange smile.

Then I remembered Hazel's poem — *Twenty-five eyeballs rolling on the floor, Twenty-five ghostly hands knocking on the door.* Oh, no! First my marbles rolled away. Now my rocks were knocking. Had Hazel put a spell on my things? I didn't want to find out. I jumped up. I ran outside to the yard. I threw those twenty-five knocking rocks away!

There was one problem. Now I only had fifty things left in my collection. What was I going to do now?

CHAPTER THREE
Creepy Crawling Critters

I sat down on a bench. Maybe I could hide out here until school was over.

Then I felt a cold breeze on my neck. I turned my head. Glenda was there. She must have come out after me.

Glenda had hair as white as snow. She always wore white dresses. Her skin was very, very pale. Sometimes I thought I could see right through her.

Just like a ghost.

Glenda put her hand on my arm. At least I think she did. I couldn't really feel it.

"What's the matter, Jane?" she asked me.

"I brought in one hundred of my favorite things to show the class," I said sadly. "But now I only have fifty left."

I looked at my last two boxes.

"See," I said. "I have twenty-five bows. And twenty-five seashells. That's only fifty."

Glenda picked up a shiny white bow. "Ooh, these are so pretty," Glenda said. "You have to show them to the class."

"But it's not the fiftieth day of school," I pointed out. "I need fifty more things to make one hundred."

Glenda giggled. "Maybe you could show them twice!" she said.

I thought about it. It was a pretty good idea.

"Thanks, Glenda," I said. "Maybe I will try that. I'll explain everything to Ms. Batley."

I felt better already.

But not for long. I should have known.

Dave, Wally, and Hazel walked out into the yard.

"Guess what?" Wally cried out. "Hazel is going to finish her poem for us. Do you want to hear it?"

Uh-oh, I thought. There was something creepy about that poem.

"Uh, I need to go," I said.

But Hazel did not give me a chance. She started to talk in that spooky voice again.

Twenty-five eyeballs rolling on the floor,
Twenty-five ghostly hands knocking on the door,
Twenty-five tiny bats flapping in the air,
Twenty-five creepy critters crawling everywhere!
These one hundred spooky things will give
     you all a scare.

Hazel raised her arms on the last line. Her green eyes gleamed.

"That was great, Hazel," Dave said. "It's too bad you didn't get to say the whole thing in class."

"Yes," Hazel said. She looked right at me. "It *is* too bad."

Goose bumps popped up on my arms. Flapping bats. Creepy critters. That poem was spooky, all right. What scary thing would happen next?

I did not have to wait long to find out.

16

A gust of wind blew across the yard. The wind picked up the bows in my box. The bows swirled and twirled in the air.

They flapped and fluttered.

Just like bats! "Oh, no!" I cried. Now what was I going to do? I tried to catch them. I ran all over the yard. Dave and Wally and Glenda tried, too.

Hazel just watched us. She had a strange smile on her face.

We could not catch the bows. The wind blew them away. I couldn't find a single one.

I walked back to the bench.

"At least I have my shells," I said. I picked up the box. It was empty!

"My shells!" I yelled. "They are gone!"

"What's that?" asked Dave. He pointed down.

My shells were all over the ground. They seemed to be moving.

Just like crawling critters.

"It must be the wind," Glenda said. But I did not feel the wind anymore.

We tried to grab the shells. But they were moving too fast. They seemed to vanish one by one.

Flapping bats. Creepy crawling critters.

It was Hazel's poem. I knew it. It was some kind of spell.

I looked at Hazel. She wasn't smiling anymore. She looked worried, just like the other kids.

"Oh, no, Jane," Hazel said. "What are you going to do?"

"I don't know," I said. "I just hope Ms. Batley understands."

"You should see her when she gets angry," said Wally. "It's pretty scary."

Of course. Vampires probably get angry all the time. And Ms. Batley was a vampire. Probably.

"I'll be careful," I said. "I'll watch my neck."

For once, the other kids looked at me like *I* was weird.

CHAPTER FOUR

Saved by a Story

The bell rang. It was time to go back inside. My legs were shaking. I could hardly walk. What was I going to do about my project? I had to think of something — fast!

I sat down at my desk.

"I hope everyone had a nice lunch," Ms. Batley said. "Now let's continue with our presentations. Where did we leave off?" Ms. Batley looked around the room.

"Ah, yes. Hazel, would you please finish your poem?" Ms. Batley asked.

Hazel smiled and walked up to the front of the classroom.

I covered my ears. I did not want to hear that creepy poem again.

Ms. Batley called on Glenda next. Good. That would give me more time to think.

Glenda slowly walked up to the front of the classroom. She spoke so quietly, I could barely hear her. I leaned forward in my seat.

20

"I will blow one hundred breaths," Glenda whispered.

"I hope she doesn't faint!" I heard Wally say.

Glenda took a deep breath. Then she started to blow. And blow. And blow. Each breath she blew was colder than the next. Not just plain cold — icy cold.

Freezing cold!

My teeth began to chatter. The hairs on my arms stood straight up. Just when I couldn't take it anymore, Glenda stopped. She had reached 100.

"Th-thank you, Gl-Glenda," Ms. Batley chattered. "Now we will hear from Jane."

I sat frozen in my seat. Really.

"Jane," Ms. Batley said again. "Jane Plain. Please come up front and share with us."

Slowly, I got up. I walked to the front of the classroom. I still didn't know what I was going to do!

Finally, I reached the front of the room. I looked at all the kids. They all looked back at me.

"Go ahead, Jane," Ms. Batley told me. "We are waiting."

I took a deep breath. "Well," I began. "Once I had a collection of my most favorite things. I had twenty-five of my best marbles, twenty-five cool rocks from all over the world, twenty-five bows of different colors, and twenty-five seashells I found on the beach. One hundred in all."

Okay, I thought. *I'm talking, but what am I going to say*

next? I looked over at Glenda. She was resting her head on her desk. I guess she was tired from blowing all those breaths. I looked over at Hazel. She gave me a little smile.

I went on with my story. "First, my marbles rolled away. I only had seventy-five of my favorite things left. Then my rocks rolled away, too. I only had fifty of my favorite things left. Next, a strong wind came along and blew my bows away. I ran after my bows, but I could not catch any of them. After that, I only had twenty-five of my favorite things left. And when I looked for my seashells, they were gone, too. I was left with nothing. Nothing at all."

I looked down at the ground. *Ms. Batley will never believe me,* I thought.

Then I heard clapping. I looked up.

Ms. Batley was clapping. And so was the rest of the class.

"That was excellent, Jane," Ms. Batley said. "A number story for the 100th day of school. And you used subtraction, too. Very, very nice."

Did she say nice? I could not believe it. I guess I was not in trouble after all.

I looked at Ms. Batley and smiled. "Thank you," I said.

The rest of the kids gave their presentations. Then Ms. Batley told us she had a surprise for us. A 100th-day-of-school surprise.

"Now close your eyes, everyone," Ms. Batley said.

I closed my eyes. I heard the classroom door shut. What was Ms. Batley going to surprise us with? One hundred slimy snakes?

I heard Ms. Batley come back in. "Okay, class. You can open your eyes now."

We opened our eyes. "Wow!" everyone said at the same time.

The classroom was filled with food. Party food! There were 100 cupcakes, 100 pieces of candy, 100 bags of chips, 100 cans of soda, and 100 cups of ice cream.

Ms. Batley smiled at us. "Since there are twenty-five

people in this classroom, how much does everyone have to eat to finish all the food?"

"Four of everything!" we all shouted.

"Great!" Ms. Batley said. "And I don't want to see any leftovers."

Everyone ran for the food. I hoped I wouldn't get a stomachache. As I was eating my fourth cupcake, Hazel walked up to me.

"I have a surprise for you, Jane," she said.

A surprise? I wasn't sure I wanted to find out what it was.

Hazel pulled me over to her desk. "Here you go," she said. And she handed me four separate boxes. My four boxes. With my most favorite things inside! My marbles. My rocks. My bows. My seashells. They were all there.

"I saw how upset you were when you lost your things," Hazel told me. "So I got them back for you."

"How . . ." I started to ask her, but I stopped. I really didn't want to know how she got my things back. I was just glad to have them.

"Thanks, Hazel," I said.

Hazel shrugged her shoulders. "No problem. I'd do anything for a friend."

A friend, I thought. Hazel might be a witch, but she was still my friend.

I took her hand. "Come on," I said. "I still have lots more to eat. I don't want Ms. Batley to get angry."

Hazel laughed. "Oh, Jane. You're so silly. Ms. Batley doesn't really expect us to eat everything. We'd be sick to our stomachs!"

"I know," I said, although I really didn't. I guess I'll never be sure of anything in this spooky school!